New York Pratt manufacturing company

A Paradise of Daintie Devices

A Collection of Poems, Songs, Ballads

New York Pratt manufacturing company

A Paradise of Daintie Devices
A Collection of Poems, Songs, Ballads

ISBN/EAN: 9783744787840

Printed in Europe, USA, Canada, Australia, Japan

Cover: Foto ©Andreas Hilbeck / pixelio.de

More available books at **www.hansebooks.com**

I love a ballad but even too well; if it be doleful matter, merrily set down, or a very pleasant thing indeed, and sung lamentably.

Shakespeare—Winter's Tale, Act IV., Sc. 3.

I have a passion for ballads. * * * They are the gypsy-children of song, born under green hedgerows, in the leafy lanes and by-paths of literature,—in the genial summer time.

Longfellow—Hyperion, Bk. II., Ch. II.

A careless song, with a little nonsense in it, now and then does not misbecome a monarch.

Horace Walpole—Letter to Sir Horace Mann. 1770.

Now, good Cesario, but that piece of song,
That old and antique song we heard last night;
Methought it did relieve my passion much,
More than light airs and recollected terms,
Of these most brisk and giddy-paced times:
Come; but one verse.

Shakespeare—Twelfth Night, Act II., Sc. 4.

A PARADISE of

DAINTIE DEVICES.

A Collection of { Poems, Songs, Ballads.

By Various Hands.

Old-fashioned poetry, but choicely good.

Izaak Walton—Complete Angler.

¶ AT NEW YORK.

Imprinted for

Charles Pratt & Co.

At 46 Broadway, near Trinity Church-Yard.

CHRISTMAS, 1882.

It (poesy) was ever thought to have some participation of divineness, because it doth raise and erect the mind, by submitting the shews of things to the desires of the mind.

Lord Bacon—Advancement of Learning, Bk. II.

Verse sweetens toil, however rude the sound ;
All at her work the village-maiden sings,
Nor while she turns the giddy wheel around,
Revolves the sad vicissitudes of things.

Gifford—Contemplation.

Poetry is older than prose. Of this we have what may be called paleonto-logical proof in the structure of all languages. Our every-day speech is fossil poetry. Words which are now dead were once alive. The farther we recede and the lower we descend, the more these wonderful petrifactions of old forms of poetic thought and feeling abound.

Abraham Coles—The Evangel—Introduction.

A verse may find him who a sermon flies,
And turn delight into a sacrifice.

George Herbert—The Temple—The Church Porch.

To all who shall receive this
Book, whether they be patrons
of ours already, or shall
become such hereafter.

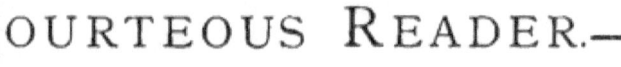OURTEOUS READER.—
*As this little book shall
cost thee nothing, save the
small time necessary for
its perusal, which most people can
very well spare, we will make no
apology to thee for the compiling of
it. The truth is, we liked that good
old custom—the exchanging of gifts
at the Christmas season—and, having profited from your patronage,*

were anxious, after this fashion, to express our appreciation and thanks.

We pretend to no wit or learning in the selections we have made, being guided therein, for the most part, by what we liked, rather than by any special erudition; yet we believe we have made such a choice as will please most and offend none. It would, indeed, be remarkable if some of the pieces to be found herein were not familiar already; still a few, we are sure, will here be made known to thee for the first time. Sufficit! What we have gathered we now present to thee, and at the same time offer our best wishes for

A MERRIE CHRISTMAS!

A Paradise of Daintie Devices.

Welcome, Merry Christmas.

B E merry all, be merry all,
　With holly dress the festive hall,
　Prepare the song, the feast, the ball,
　　To welcome Merry Christmas.

And oh! remember, gentles gay,
For you who bask in fortune's ray,
The year is all a holiday,—
　　The poor have only Christmas.

When you with velvets mantled o'er
Defy December's tempest's roar,
Oh! spare one garment from your store,
      To clothe the poor at Christmas.

When you the costly banquet deal
To guests, who never famine feel,
Oh! spare one morsel from your meal,
      To feed the poor at Christmas.

When gen'rous wine your care controls,
And gives new joy to happiest souls,
Oh! spare one goblet from your bowls,
      To cheer the poor at Christmas.

So shall each note of mirth appear
More sweet to Heaven than praise or prayer,
And Angels, in their carols there,
      Shall bless the poor at Christmas.

Old Carol.

King

ᕱ King Witlaf's Drinking Horn.

WITLAF, a king of the Saxons,
    Ere yet his last he breathed,
To the merry monks of Croyland
    His drinking-horn bequeathed,—

That, whenever they sat at their revels,
    And drank from the golden bowl,
They might remember the donor,
    And breathe a prayer for his soul.

So sat they once at Christmas,
    And bade the goblet pass;
In their beards the red wine glistened
    Like dewdrops in the grass.

They drank to the soul of Witlaf,
    They drank to Christ the Lord,
And to each of the Twelve Apostles,
    Who had preached His holy word.

They drank to the Saints and Martyrs
    Of the dismal days of yore,
And as soon as the horn was empty
    They remembered one Saint more.

And

And the reader droned from the pulpit,
    Like the murmur of many bees,
The legend of good Saint Guthlac,
    And Saint Basil's homilies ;

Till the great bells of the convent,
    From their prison in the tower,
Guthlac and Bartholomæus,
    Proclaimed the midnight hour.

And the Yule log cracked in the chimney,
    And the Abbot bowed his head,
And the flamelets flapped and flickered,
    But the Abbot was stark and dead.

Yet still in his pallid fingers
    He clutched the golden bowl,
In which, like a pearl dissolving,
    Had sunk and dissolved his soul.

But not for this their revels
    The jovial monks forbore,
For they cried, " Fill high the goblet !
    We must drink to one Saint more ! "

H. W. Longfellow.

Song

❧ *Song.*

HEARS not my *Phyllis* how the birds
    Their feathered mates salute ?
    They tell their passion in their words ;
    Must I alone be mute ?
Phyllis, without frown or smile,
Sat and knotted all the while.

The god of love in thy bright eyes
    Does like a tyrant reign ;
But in thy heart a child he lies,
    Without his dart or flame.
Phyllis, without frown or smile,
Sat and knotted all the while.

So many months in silence past,
    And yet in raging love,
Might well deserve one word at last
    My passion should approve.
Phyllis, without frown or smile,
Sat and knotted all the while.

Must

Must then your faithful swain expire,
   And not one look obtain,
Which he, to soothe his fond desire,
   Might pleasingly explain?
Phyllis, without frown or smile,
Sat and knotted all the while.

          Sir Charles Sedley, 1639—1701.

Upon a Child that Died.

HERE she lies, a pretty bud,
   Lately made of flesh and blood:
   When, as soon, fell fast asleep,
As her little eyes did peep.
Give her strewings; but not stir
The earth, that lightly covers her.

          Robert Herrick, 1591—1674.

Love

¶ *Love and Age.*

I PLAY'D with you 'mid cowslips blowing,
　　When I was six and you were four;
　When garlands weaving, flower-balls throwing,
　　Were pleasures soon to please no more.
Thro' groves and meads, o'er grass and heather,
　With little playmates, to and fro,
We wander'd hand in hand together;
　But that was sixty years ago.

You grew a lovely, roseate maiden,
　And still our early love was strong;
Still with no care our days were laden,
　They glided joyously along;
And I did love you very dearly,—
　How dearly, words want power to show;
I thought your heart was touched as nearly,—
　But that was fifty years ago.

Then

Then other lovers came around you,
  Your beauty grew from year to year,
And many a splendid circle found you
  The center of its glittering sphere.
I saw you then, first vows forsaking,
  On rank and wealth your hand bestow ;
Oh, then I thought my heart was breaking,—
  But that was forty years ago.

And I lived on to wed another ;
  No cause she gave me to repine ;
And when I heard you were a mother,
  I did not wish the children mine.
My own young flock, in fair progression,
  Made up a pleasant Christmas row :
My joy in them was past expression,—
  But that was thirty years ago.

You grew a matron plump and comely,
  You dwelt in fashion's brightest blaze ;
My earthly lot was far more homely ;
  But I, too, had my festal days.
No merrier eyes have ever glisten'd
  Around the hearth-stone's wintry glow,
Than when my youngest child was christen'd,—
  But that was twenty years ago.

Time passed. My eldest girl was married,
  And I am now a grandsire gray ;
One pet of four years old I've carried
  Among the wild-flower'd meads to play.

In our old fields of childish pleasure,
   Where now, as then, the cowslips blow,
She fills her basket's ample measure,—
   And that is not ten years ago.

But tho' first love's impassion'd blindness
   Has pass'd away in colder light,
I still have thought of you with kindness,
   And shall do, till our last good-night.
The ever-rolling silent hours
   Will bring a time we shall not know,
When our young days of gathering flowers
   Will be a hundred years ago.

                Thomas L. Peacock.

On

¶ *On Drinking.*

OUT OF ANACREON.

THE thirsty earth soaks up the rain,
   And drinks, and gapes for drink again;
   The plants suck in the earth, and are
With constant drinking fresh and fair.
The sea itself, which one would think
Should have but little need to drink,
Drinks twice ten thousand rivers up,
So filled that they o'erflow the cup.
The busy sun (and one would guess
By 's drunken fiery face no less)
Drinks up the sea, and, when he 's done,
The moon and stars drink up the sun.
They drink and dance by their own light,
They drink and revel all the night;
Nothing in Nature's sober found,
But an eternal health goes round.
Fill up the bowl, then, fill it high,
Fill all the glasses there, for why
Should every creature drink but I;
Thou man of morals, tell me why?

       Abraham Cowley, 1618—1667.

      Robin

Robin Hood and Allin-a-Dale.

COME, listen to me, you gallants so free,
 All you that love mirth for to hear,
And I will tell you of a bold outláw
 That lived in Nottinghamshire.

As Robin Hood in the forest stood,
 All under the greenwood tree,
There he was aware of a brave young man,
 As fine as fine might be.

The youngster was clothed in scarlet red,
 In scarlet fine and gay;
And he did frisk it over the plain,
 And chanted a roundelay.

As Robin Hood next morning stood
 Amongst the leaves so gay,
Then did he espy the same young man
 Come drooping along the way.

The scarlet he wore the day before
 It was clean cast away;
And at every step he fetched a sigh,—
 "Alack, and a well-a-day!"

Then

Then steppéd forth brave Little John,
  And Midge, the miller's son,
Which made the young man bend his bow,
  When as he saw them come.

" Stand off, stand off ! " the young man said ;
  " What is your will with me ? "
" You must come before our master straight,
  Under yon greenwood tree."

And when he came bold Robin before,
  Robin asked him courteously,
" Oh, hast thou any money to spare
  For my merry men and me ? "

" I have no money," the young man said,
  " But five shillings and a ring ;
And that I have kept this seven long years,
  To have it at my wedding.

" Yesterday I should have married a maid,
  But she soon from me was ta'en,
And chosen to be an old knight's delight,
  Whereby my poor heart is slain."

" What is thy name ? " then said Robin Hood ;
  " Come, tell me without any fail."
" By the faith of my body," then said the young man ;
  " My name it is Allin-a-Dale."

                                    " What

" What wilt thou give me," said Robin Hood,
 " In ready gold or fee,
 To help thee to thy true love again,
  And deliver her unto thee?"

" I have no money," then quoth the young man,
 " No ready gold nor fee;
 But I will swear upon a book
  Thy true servánt for to be."

" How many miles is it to thy true love?
 Come, tell me without guile."
" By the faith of my body," then said the young man,
 " It is but five little mile."

 Then Robin he hasted over the plain,
  He did neither stint nor bin,
 Until he came unto the church
  Where Allin should keep his wedding.

" What hast thou here?" the bishop then said,
 " I prithee now tell unto me."
" I am a bold harper," quoth Robin Hood,
 And the best in the north countree."

" O welcome, O welcome!" the bishop he said,
 " That music best pleaseth me."
" You shall have no music," quoth Robin Hood,
 " Till the bride and bridegroom I see."

         With

With that came in a wealthy knight,
   Which was both grave and old ;
And after him a finikin lass
   Did shine like the glistering gold.

" This is not a fit match," quoth bold Robin Hood,
   " That you do seem to make here ;
For since we are come into the church,
   The bride shall choose her own dear."

Then Robin Hood put his horn to his mouth,
   And blew blasts two or three,
And four-and-twenty bowmen bold,
   Came leaping o'er the lea.

And when they came into the church-yard,
   Marching all in a row,
The very first man was Allin-a-Dale
   To give bold Robin his bow.

" This is thy true love," Robin he said,
   " Young Allin, as I hear say ;
And you shall be married at this same time,
   Before we depart away."

" That shall not be," the bishop he said,
   " For thy word shall not stand ;
They shall be three times asked in church,
   As the law is of our land."

                                   Robin

Robin Hood pulled off the bishop's coat,
   And pulled it on Little John.
" By the faith of my body," then Robin said,
   " This cloth doth make thee a man."

When Little John went into the quire;
   The people began to laugh ;
He asked them seven times in the church,
   Lest three times should not be enough.

" Who gives me this maid ? " said Little John,
   Quoth Robin Hood, " That do I ;
And he that takes her from Allin-a-Dale,
   Full dearly he shall her buy."

And thus having end of this merry wedding,
   The bride looked like a queen ;
And so they returned to the merry greenwood,
   Amongst the leaves so green.

                        Old Ballad.

On

🙟 *On a Girdle.*

THAT which her slender waist confined
Shall now my joyful temples bind;
　No monarch but would give his crown
His arms might do what this has done.

It was my heaven's extremest sphere,
The pale which held that lovely dear; ˙
My joy, my grief, my hope, my love,
Did all within this circle move.

A narrow compass, and yet there
Dwelt all that's good and all that's fair;
Give me but what this riband bound,
Take all the rest the sun goes round.

Edmund Waller, 1605—1687.

Across

¶ *Across the Street.*

WITH lash on cheek, she comes and goes
I watch her when she little knows:
I wonder if she dreams of it.
Sitting and working at my rhymes,
I weave into my verse, at times
Her sunny hair, or gleams of it.

Upon her window-ledge is set
A box of flowering mignonette ;
Morning and eve she tends to them —
The senseless flowers, that do not care
About that loosened strand of hair,
As prettily she bends to them.

If I could once contrive to get
Into that box of mignonette
Some morning when she tends to them —
She comes! I see the rich blood rise
From throat to cheek!—down go the eyes
Demurely, as she bends to them!

Thomas Bailey Aldrich.

❧ *Sephestia's Song to her Child.*

WEEP not, my wanton, smile upon my knee,
When thou art old, there's grief enough for
thee.
Mother's wag, pretty boy,
Father's sorrow, father's joy.
When thy father first did see
Such a boy by him and me,
He was glad, I was woe;
Fortune changed made him so
When he left his pretty boy,
Last his sorrow, first his joy.

Weep not, my wanton, smile upon my knee,
When thou art old, there's grief enough for thee.
Streaming tears that never stint,
Like pearl drops from a flint,
Fell by course from his eyes,
That one another's place supplies:

Thus

Thus he grieved in every part,
Tears of blood fell from his heart,
When he left his pretty boy,
Father's sorrow, father's joy.

Weep not, my wanton, smile upon my knee,
When thou art old, there's grief enough for thee.
The wanton smiled, father wept;
Mother cried, baby leapt:
More he crowed, more we cried,
Nature could not sorrow hide.
He must go, he must kiss
Child and mother, baby bless:
For he left his pretty boy,
Father's sorrow, father's joy.

Weep not, my wanton, smile upon my knee,
When thou art old, there's grief enough for thee.

From " Menaphon," 1589, by Robert Greene.

Please

¶ *"Please to Ring the Belle."*

I'LL tell you a story that's not in Tom Moore:
  Young love likes to knock at a pretty girl's door:
  So he called upon Lucy—'twas just ten o'clock—
Like a spruce single man, with a smart double knock.

Now a hand-maid, whatever her fingers be at,
Will run like a puss when she hears a *rat*-tat:
So Lucy ran up—and in two seconds more
Had question'd the stranger and answer'd the door.

The meeting was bliss; but the parting was woe;
For the moment will come when such comers must go.
So she kissed him and whisper'd—poor innocent
    thing—
"The next time you come, love, pray come with a
    ring."

                Thomas Hood, 1798— 1845.

                                    Sonnet.

❧ *Sonnet.*

ALEXIS, here she stayed; among these pines,
Sweet hermitress, she did alone repair;
Here did she spread the treasure of her hair,
More rich than that brought from the Colchian mines;
She sat her by these muskèd eglantines —
The happy place the print seems yet to bear;
Her voice did sweeten here thy sugared lines,
To which winds, trees, beasts, birds, did lend their ear;
Me here she first perceived, and here a morn
Of bright carnations did o'erspread her face;
Here did she sigh, here first my hopes were born,
And I first got a pledge of promised grace;
But ah! what served it to be happy so
Sith passèd pleasures double but new woe?

William Drummond, 1585 — 1649.

Sonnet.

 *Sonnet.*

A ROSE, as fair as ever saw the North,
Grew in a little garden all alone:
A sweeter flower did Nature ne'er put forth,
Nor fairer garden yet was never known.
The maidens danced about it morn and noon,
And learnèd bards of it their ditties made;
The nimble fairies, by the pale-faced moon,
Watered the root, and kissed her pretty shade.
But, well-a-day! the gardener careless grew,
The maids and fairies both were kept away,
And in a drought the caterpillars threw
Themselves upon the bud and every spray.
God shield the stock! If heaven send no supplies,
The fairest blossom of the garden dies.

William Browne, 1588—1643.

Kitty

¶ Kitty of Coleraine.

A^S beautiful Kitty one morning was tripping,
　　With a pitcher of milk from the fair of Coleraine,
　　When she saw me she stumbled, the pitcher it
　　　tumbled,
　　And all the sweet butter-milk water'd the plain.

O, what shall I do now, 'twas looking at you now,
　　Sure, sure, such a pitcher I'll ne'er meet again,
'Twas the pride of my dairy, O, Barney M'Leary,
　　You're sent as a plague to the girls of Coleraine.

I sat down beside her,— and gently did chide her,
　　That such a misfortune should give her such pain,
A kiss then I gave her,— before I did leave her,
　　She vow'd for such pleasure she'd break it again.

　　　　　　　　　　　　　　　　　　　　　　　'Twas

'Twas hay-making season, I can't tell the reason,
   Misfortunes will never come single,—that's plain,
For, very soon after poor Kitty's disaster,
   The devil a pitcher was whole in Coleraine.

Unknown.

YYYYYYYYYYYYYYYYYYYYYYYYYYY

L ORD ERSKINE, on woman presuming to rail,
   Calls a wife " a tin canister tied to one's tail ";
   And fair Lady Anne, while the subject he car-
      ries on,
Seems hurt at his lordship's degrading comparison.
But wherefore degrading? consider'd aright,
A canister's polish'd, and useful, and bright:
And should dirt its original purity hide,
That's the fault of the puppy to whom it is tied.

Richard B. Sheridan.

A

A Pastoral Song between Phyllis
and Amaryllis, two Nymphs, each answering other line for line.

PHYLLIS.

FIE on the slights that men devise
  Heigh-ho, silly slights;
When simple Maids they would entice,
  Maids are young men's chief delights.

AMARYLLIS.

Nay, women they witch with their eyes,
  Eyes like beams of burning sun:
And men once caught, they soon despise;
  So are Shepherds oft undone.

PHYLLIS.

If any young man win a maid,
  Happy man is he;
By trusting him she is betrayed;
  Fie upon such treachery.

                                        Amaryllis.

AMARYLLIS.

If Maids win young men with their guiles
    Heigh-ho, guileful grief:
They deal like weeping crocodiles
    That murder men without relief.

PHYLLIS.

I know a simple country Hind
    Heigh-ho, silly swain:
To whom fair Daphne provèd kind,
    Was he not kind to her again?
He vowed by Pan with many an oath,
    Heigh-ho, Shepherds' God is he:
Yet since hath changed, and broke his troth,
    Troth-plight broke will plaguèd be.

AMARYLLIS.

She had deceived many a swain,
    Fie on false deceit:
And plighted troth to them in vain,
    There can be no grief more great,
Her measure was with measure paid,
    Heigh-ho, heigh-ho, equal meed:
She was beguil'd that had betrayed,
    So shall all deceivers speed.

PHYLLIS.

If every Maid were like to me,
    Heigh-ho, hard of heart:
Both love and lovers scorn'd should be,
    Scorners shall be sure of smart.

                   Amaryllis.

AMARYLLIS.

If every Maid were of my mind,
  Heigh-ho, heigh-ho, lovely sweet :
They to their lovers should prove kind,
  Kindness is for Maidens meet.

HYLLIS.

Methinks love is an idle toy,
  Heigh-ho, busy pain :
Both wit and sense it doth annoy,
  Both sense and wit thereby we gain.

AMARYLLIS.

Tush ! Phyllis, cease, be not so coy,
  Heigh-ho, heigh-ho, coy disdain :
I know you love a Shepherd's boy,
  Fie ! that Maidens so should fain !

PHYLLIS.

Well, Amaryllis, now I yield,
  Shepherds, pipe aloud :
Love conquers both in town and field,
  Like a tyrant, fierce and proud.
The evening star is up, ye see ;
  Vesper shines ; we must away ;
    Would every lover might agree,
    So we end our roundelay.

Henry Constable. In "England's Helicon," 1600.
Song.

¶ *Song.*

A WET sheet and a flowing sea,
  A wind that follows fast,
And fills the white and rustling sail,
  And bends the gallant mast;
And bends the gallant mast, my boys,
  While, like the eagle free,
Away the good ship flies, and leaves
  Old England on the lee.

Oh, for a soft and gentle wind!
  I hear a fair one cry;
But give to me the snoring breeze,
  And white waves heaving high;
And white waves heaving high, my boys,
  The good ship tight and free,—
The world of waters is our home,
  And merry men are we.

There's

There's tempest in yon hornèd moon,
  And lightning in yon cloud;
And hark, the music, mariners,
  The wind is piping loud!
The wind is piping loud, my boys,
  The lightning flashing free,—
While the hollow oak our palace is,
  Our heritage the sea.

Allan Cunningham, 1784 — 1842.

O GIN my 'love were yon red rose,
    That grows upon the castle wa'!
  And I mysel, a drap of dew,
Into her bonny breast to fa'!

O, there beyond expression blest
  I'd feast on beauty a' the night;
Seal'd on her silk-saft falds to rest,
  Till flyed awa' by Phœbus light.

From Herd's Scottish Songs, 1776.

In

In School-Days.

STILL sits the school-house by the road,
    A ragged beggar sunning;
Around it still the sumachs grow,
And blackberry vines are running.

Within, the master's desk is seen,
    Deep scarred by raps official;
The warping floor, the battered seats,
    The jack-knife's carved initial;

The charcoal frescos on its wall;
    Its door's worn sill betraying
The feet that, creeping slow to school,
    Went storming out to playing!

Long years ago, a winter sun
    Shone over it at setting;
Lit up its western window-panes,
    And low eaves' icy fretting.

It

It touched the tangled golden curls,
  And brown eyes full of grieving,
Of one who still her steps delayed
  When all the school were leaving.

For near her stood the little boy
  Her childish favor singled;
His cap pulled low upon a face
  Where pride and shame were mingled.

Pushing with restless feet the snow
  To right and left, he lingered;
As restlessly her tiny hands
  The blue-checked apron fingered.

He saw her lift her eyes; he felt
  The soft hand's light caressing,
And heard the tremble of her voice,
  As if a fault confessing.

" I'm sorry that I spelt the word:
  I hate to go above you,
Because,"—the brown eyes lower fell,—
  " Because, you see, I love you!"

Still memory to a gray-haired man
  That sweet child-face is showing.
Dear girl! the grasses on her grave
  Have forty years been growing!

                      He

He lives to learn, in life's hard school,
  How few who pass above him
Lament their triumph and his loss,
  Like her,—because they love him.

                   John Greenleaf Whittier.

*How Violets came Blue.*

L OVE on a day, wise poets tell,
  Some time in wrangling spent,
  Whether the Violets should excel,
Or she, in sweetest scent.

But Venus having lost the day,
  Poor girls! she fell on you;
And beat ye so as some dare say,
  Her blows did make ye blue.

           Robert Herrick, 1591 — 1674.

Minerva's

¶ *Minerva's Thimble.*

YOUNG Jessica sat all the day,
    With heart o'er idle love-thoughts pining,
    Her needle bright beside her lay,
So active once!—now idly shining.
Ah, Jessy, 'tis in idle hearts
    That love and mischief are most nimble;
The safest shield against the darts
    Of Cupid, is Minerva's thimble.

The child, who with a magnet plays,
    Well knowing all its arts, so wily,
The tempter near a needle lays,
    And laughing, says, "We'll steal it slily."
The needle, having naught to do,
    Is pleased to let the magnet wheedle,
Till closer, closer come the two,
    And off, at length, elopes the needle.

 Now

Now, had this needle turned its eye
    To some gay reticule's construction,
It ne'er had strayed from duty's tie,
    Nor felt the magnet's sly seduction.
Thus, girls, would you keep quiet hearts,
    Your snowy fingers must be nimble;
The safest shield against the darts
    Of Cupid, is Minerva's thimble.

                    Thomas Moore, 1780 — 1852.

Epitaph in Croyland Abbey.

MAN'S life is like unto a winter's day,—
    Some break their fast and so depart away.
        Others stay dinner, then depart full fed:
The longest age but sups and goes to bed.
    O, reader, then behold and see,
    As we are now, so thou must be!

                    Unknown.

                                    The

¶ *The Hare and Many Friends.*

FRIENDSHIP, like love, is but a name,
  Unless to one you stint the flame.
  The child whom many fathers share,
Hath seldom known a father's care.
'Tis thus in friendship: who depend
On many, rarely find a friend.
  A Hare, who, in a civil way,
Complied with everything, like Gay,
Was known by all the bestial train
Who haunt the wood or graze the plain:
Her care was never to offend,
And every creature was her friend.
  As forth she went at early dawn,
To taste the dew-besprinkled lawn,
Behind she hears the hunter's cries,
And from the deep-mouthed thunder flies.
She starts, she stops, she pants for breath;
She hears the near advance of death;

She

She doubles, to mislead the hound,
And measures back her mazy round;
Till, fainting in the public way,
Half dead with fear she gasping lay.

What transport in her bosom grew
When first the Horse appeared in view!

"Let me," says she, "your back ascend,
And owe my safety to a friend.
You know my feet betray my flight:
To friendship every burden's light."

The Horse replied, "Poor honest Puss,
It grieves my heart to see thee thus:
Be comforted; relief is near,
For all your friends are in the rear."

She next the stately Bull implored,
And thus replied the mighty lord:
"Since every beast alive can tell
That I sincerely wish you well,
I may without offense pretend
To take the freedom of a friend.
Love calls me hence; a favorite cow
Expects me near yon barley-mow;
And when a lady's in the case,
You know, all other things give place.
To leave you thus might seem unkind,
But, see, the Goat is just behind."

The Goat remarked her pulse was high,
Her languid head, her heavy eye:
"My back," says he, "may do you harm;
The Sheep's at hand, and wool is warm."

The

The Sheep was feeble, and complained
His sides a load of wool sustained;
Said he was slow; confessed his fears,
For hounds eat sheep as well as hares.
  She now the trotting Calf addressed
To save from death a friend distressed
  "Shall I," says he, "of tender age,
In this important care engage?
Older and abler passed you by.
How strong are those! how weak am I!
Should I presume to bear you hence,
Those friends of mine may take offense.
Excuse me, then; you know my heart;
But dearest friends, alas! must part.
How shall we all lament! Adieu;
For, see, the hounds are just in view."

From Fables by John Gay, 1688 — 1732.

Cupid

¶ *Cupid Mistaken.*

A S after noon, one summer's day,
    Venus stood bathing in a river;
    Cupid a-shooting went that way,
New strung his bow, new fill'd his quiver.

With skill he chose his sharpest dart,
    With all his might his bow he drew;
Swift to his beauteous parent's heart
    The too well-guided arrow flew.

"I faint! I die!" the goddess cried;
    "O, cruel, couldst thou find none other,
To wrack thy spleen on? Parricide!
    Like Nero, thou hast slain thy mother."

Poor Cupid sobbing scarce could speak;
    "Indeed, mamma, I did not know ye:
Alas! how easy my mistake;
    I took you for your likeness, Chloe."

                       Matthew Prior, 1664 — 1721.

                                       Sonnet.

𝔞❧ *Sonnet.*

TO one who has been long in city pent
'Tis very sweet to look into the fair
And open face of heaven,—to breathe a prayer
Full in the smile of the blue firmament.
Who is more happy, when, with heart's content,
Fatigued he sinks into some pleasant lair
Of wavy grass, and reads a debonair
And gentle tale of love and languishment
Returning home at evening, with an ear
Catching the notes of Philomel,—an eye
Watching the sailing cloudlet's bright career,
He mourns that day so soon has glided by:
Even like the passage of an angel's tear
That falls through the clear ether silently.

John Keats, 1795 — 1821.

The

¶ *The Children in the Wood: or, the Norfolk Gentleman's Last Will and Testament.*

NOW ponder well, you parents deare,
    These words which I shall write;
    A doleful story you shall heare,
  In time brought forth to light.
A gentleman of good account
  In Norfolk dwelt of late,
Who did in honour far surmount
  Most men of his estate.

Sore sicke he was, and like to dye,
  No helpe his life could save;
His wife by him as sicke did lye,
  And both possest one grave.
No love between these two was lost,
  Each was to other kinde;
In love they liv'd, in love they dyed,
  And left two babes behinde:

        The

The one a fine and pretty boy,
  Not passing three years olde;
The other a girl more young than he
  And fram'd in beautyes molde.
The father left his little son,
  As plainlye doth appeare,
When he to perfect age should come,
  Three hundred poundes a year.

And to his little daughter Jane
  Five hundred poundes in gold,
To be paid downe on marriage-day,
  Which might not be controll'd:
But if the children chance to dye,
  Ere they to age should come,
Their uncle should possesse their wealth;
  For so the wille did run.

"Now, brother," said the dying man,
  "Look to my children deare;
Be good unto my boy and girl,
  No friendes else have they here.
To God and you I recommend
  My children deare this daye;
But little while be sure we have
  Within this world to staye.

"You must be father and mother both,
  And uncle all in one;
God knowes what will become of them,
  When I am dead and gone."

                                    With

With that bespake their mother deare,
  "O, brother kinde," quoth shee,
"You are the man must bring our babes
  To wealth or miserie.

"And if you keep them carefully;
  Then God will you reward;
But if you otherwise should deal,
  God will your deedes regard."
With lippes as cold as any stone,
  They kist their children small:
"God bless you both, my children deare;"
  With that the tears did fall.

These speeches then their brother spake
  To this sicke couple there;
"The keeping of your little ones,
  Sweet sister, do not feare.
God never prosper me nor mine,
  Nor aught else that I have,
If I do wrong your children deare,
  When you are layd in grave."

The parents being dead and gone,
  The children home he takes,
And brings them straite untó his house,
  Where much of them he makes.
He had not kept those pretty babes
  A twelve-month and a daye,
But, for their wealth he did devise
  To make them both awaye.

He

He bargained with two ruffians strong,
   Which were of furious mood,
That they should take these children young,
   And slaye them in a wood.
He told his wife an artful tale,
   He would the children send
To be brought up in faire London,
   With one that was his friend.

Away then went those pretty babes,
   Rejoycing at that tide,
Rejoycing with a merry minde,
   They should on cock-horse ride.
They prate and prattle pleasantly,
   As they rode on the waye,
To those that should their butchers be,
   And worke their lives decaye:

So that the pretty speeche they had,
   Made Murder's heart relent:
And they that undertooke the deed,
   Full sore did now repent.
Yet one of them, more hard of heart,
   Did vowe to do his charge,
Because the wretch that hired him,
   Had paid him very large.

The other wont agree thereto,
   So here they fall to strife;
With one another they did fight,
   About the children's life:

                And

And he that was of mildest mood,
  Did slaye the other there,
Within an unfrequented wood;
  The babes did quake with fear.

He took the children by the hand,
  Teares standing in their eye;
And bade them straightwaye follow him,
  And look they did not crye:
And two long miles he ledd them on,
  While they for food complaine:
"Stay here," quoth he, "I'll bring you bread,
  When I come back againe."

These pretty babes, with hand in hand,
  Went wandering up and downe;
But never more could see the man
  Approaching from the town;
Their pretty lippes with blackberries,
  Were all besmeared and dyed,
And when they sawe the darksome night,
  They sat them downe and cryed.

Thus wandered these poor innocents,
  Till deathe did end their grief,
In one another's armes they dyed,
  As wanting due relief:
No burial this pretty pair
  Of any man receives,
Till Robin-red-breast piously
  Did cover them with leaves.

                                And

And now the heavy wrathe of God
  Upon their uncle fell;
Yea, fearful fiends did haunt his house,
  His conscience felt an hell:
His barnes were fir'd, his goodes consum'd,
  His lands were barren made,
His cattle dyed within the field,
  And nothing with him stay'd.

And in a voyage to Portugal
  Two of his sonnes did dye;
And to conclude, himselfe was brought
  To want and miserye:
He pawn'd and mortgaged all his land,
  Ere seven yeares came about,
And now at length this wicked act
  Did by this meanes come out:

The fellowe that did take in hand
  These children for to kill,
Was for a robbery judg'd to dye,
  Such was God's blessed will:
Who did confess the very truth,
  As here hath been display'd:
Their uncle having dyed in gaol,
  Where he for debt was layd.

You that executors be made,
  And overseers eke
Of children that be fatherless,
  And infants mild and meek;

                        Take

Take you example by this thing,
And yield to each his right,
Lest God, with such like miserye,
Your wicked minds requite.

Old Ballad, printed about 1595.

¶ *To His Soul.*

POOR little, pretty, fluttering thing,
Must we no longer live together?
And dost thou prune thy trembling wing,
To take thy flight thou know'st not whither?

Thy humorous vein, thy pleasing folly
Lie all neglected, all forgot:
And pensive, wavering, melancholy,
Thou dread'st and hop'st thou know'st not what.

Matthew Prior, 1664—1721.

The

The Poplar.

A Y, here stands the poplar, so tall and so stately,
    On whose tender rind—'twas a little one then—
    We carved her initials; though not very lately,
We think in the year eighteen hundred and ten.

Yes, here is the *G*, which proclaim'd Georgiana;
    Our heart's empress then—see, 'tis grown all askew;
And it's not without grief we perforce entertain a
    Conviction it now looks much more like a *Q*.

This should be the great *D*, too, that once stood for
        Dobbin,
    Her loved patronymic—Ah! can it be so?
Its once fair proportions, time, too, has been robbing:
    A *D?* we'll be *Deed* if it isn't an *O!*

Alas! how the soul sentimental it vexes,
    That thus on our labours stern *Chronos* should frown;
Should change our soft liquids to izzards and Xes,
    And turn true-love's alphabet all upside down!

Richard H. Barham, 1780—1845.

Song.

Song.

LET schoolmasters puzzle their brain
   With grammar, and nonsense, and learning,
   Good liquor, I stoutly maintain,
  Gives *genius* a better discerning.
Let them brag of their heathenish gods,
   Their Lethes, their Styxes, and Stygians;
Their *quis*, and their *quæs*, and their *quods*,
   They're all but a parcel of pigeons.
     Toroddle, toroddle, toroll.

When Methodist preachers come down,
   A-preaching that drinking is sinful,
I'll wager the rascals a crown,
   They always preach best with a skinful.
But when you come down with your pence,
   For a slice of their scurvy religion,
I'll leave it to all men of sense,
   But you, my good friend, are the pigeon.
     Toroddle, toroddle, toroll.

Then

Then come, put the jorum about,
   And let us be merry and clever,
Our hearts and our liquors are stout,
   Here's the Three Jolly Pigeons for ever.
Let some cry up woodcock or hare,
   Your bustards, your ducks, and your widgeons,
But of all the gay birds in the air,
   Here's a health to the Three Jolly Pigeons.
     Toroddle, toroddle, toroll.

           Oliver Goldsmith, 1728—1774.

¶ *Jenny Kiss'd Me.*

JENNY kiss'd me when we met,
   Jumping from the chair she sat in;
   Time, you thief! who love to get
Sweets into your list, put that in.
Say I'm weary, say I'm sad;
   Say that health and wealth have miss'd me;
Say I'm growing old, but add—
        Jenny kiss'd me!

     Leigh Hunt, 1784—1859.

New

New York.

NIEUW AMSTERDAM.

WHERE nowadays the Battery lies,
New York had just begun,
A new-born babe, to rub its eyes
In Sixteen-sixty-one.
They christened it Nieuw Amsterdam,
Those burghers grave and stately,
And so, with schnapps and smoke and psalm,
Lived out their lives sedately.

Two windmills topped their wooden wall,
On Stadthuys gazing down
On fort and cabbage-plots and all
The quaintly gabled town;
These flapped their wings and shifted backs,
As ancient scrolls determine,
To scare the savage Hackensacks,
Paumanks, and other vermin.

At

At night the loyal settlers lay
  Betwixt their feather-beds ;
In hose and breeches walked by day,
  And smoked and wagged their heads.
No changeful fashions came from France,
  The vrouwleins to bewilder ;
No broad-brimmed burgher spent for pants
  His every other guilder.

In petticoats of linsey-red,
  And jackets neatly kept,
The vrouws their knitting-needles sped
  And deftly spun and swept.
Few modern-school flirtations there
  Set wheels of scandal trundling,
But youths and maidens did their share
  Of staid, old-fashioned bundling.

Edmund Clarence Stedman.

To

To my Cigar.

YES, social friend, I love thee well,
  In learned doctor's spite:
    Thy cloud all other clouds dispel
And lap me in delight.

What though they tell, with phizzes long,
  My years are sooner passed!
I would reply with reason strong,
  They're sweeter while they last.

When in the lonely evening hour,
  Attended but by thee,
O'er history's varied page I pore,
  Man's fate in thine I see.

Oft as the snowy column grows,
  Then breaks and falls away,
I trace how mighty realms thus rose,
  Thus tumbled to decay.

Awhile

Awhile like thee earth's masters burn
  And smoke and fume around,
And then like thee, to ashes turn
  And mingle with the ground.

Life's but a leaf adroitly rolled,
  And Time's the wasting breath
That late or early we behold
  Gives all to dusty death.

From beggar's frieze to monarch's robe
  One common doom is passed;
Sweet Nature's works, the swelling globe,
  Must all burn out at last.

And what is he who smokes thee now?
  A little moving heap,
That soon, like thee, to fate must bow,
  With thee in dust must sleep.

But though thy ashes downward go,
  Thy essence rolls on high;
Thus when my body lieth low
  My soul shall cleave the sky.

Charles Sprague, 1791—1876.

Rosalind's

Rosalind's Madrigal.

LOVE in my bosom like a bee
  Doth suck his sweet:
    Now with his wings he plays with me,
  Now with his feet.
Within mine eyes he makes his nest,
His bed amidst my tender breast:
My kisses are his daily feast,
And yet he robs me of my rest.
  Ah, wanton, will ye?

And if I sleep, then percheth he
  With pretty flight,
And makes his pillow of my knee
  The live-long night.
Strike I my lute, he tunes the string,
He music plays if so I sing,
He lends me every lovely thing:
Yet cruel he my heart doth sting:
  Whist, wanton, still ye!

Else

Else I with roses every day
  Will whip you hence:
And bind you, when you long to play,
  For your offense.
I'll shut mine eyes to keep you in,
I'll make you fast it for your sin,
I'll count your power not worth a pin;
Alas, what hereby shall I win,
  If he gainsay me?

What if I beat the wanton boy
  With many a rod?
He will repay me with annoy,
  Because a god.
Then sit thou safely on my knee,
And let thy bower my bosom be;
Lurk in my eyes I like of thee:
O, Cupid so thou pity me,
  Spare not, but play thee.

From " Euphues Golden Legacie," 1592.
By Thomas Lodge.

John

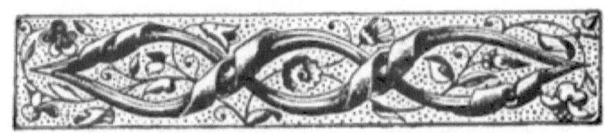

John Anderson My Jo.

JOHN ANDERSON my jo, John,
  When we were first acquent,
  Your locks were like the raven,
Your bonnie brow was brent;
But now your brow is beld, John,
  Your locks are like the snaw;
But, blessings on your frosty pow,
  John Anderson, my jo.

John Anderson my jo, John,
  We clamb the hill thegither;
And monie a cantie day, John,
  We've had wi' ane anither:
Now we maun totter down, John,
  But hand in hand we'll go,
And sleep thegither at the foot,
  John Anderson, my jo.

Robert Burns, 1759—1796.

The

¶ *The Alarméd Skipper.*

"IT WAS AN ANCIENT MARINER."

MANY a long, long year ago,
  Nantucket skippers had a plan
  Of finding out, though "lying low,"
How near New York their schooners ran.

They greased the lead before it fell,
And then, by sounding through the night,
Knowing the soil that stuck, so well,
They always guessed their reckoning right.

A skipper gray, whose eyes were dim,
Could tell, by *tasting*, just the spot;
And so below he'd "dowse the glim,"—
After, of course, his "something hot."

Snug in his berth, at eight o'clock,
This ancient skipper might be found;
No matter how his craft would rock,
He slept,—for skippers' naps are sound.

The

The watch on deck would now and then
Run down and wake him, with the lead;
He'd up, and taste, and tell the men
How many miles they went ahead.

One night, 'twas Jotham Marden's watch,
A curious wag,—the peddler's son,
And so he mused (the wanton wretch),
"To-night I'll have a grain of fun.

"We're all a set of stupid fools
To think the skipper knows by *tasting*
What ground he's on,—Nantucket schools
Don't teach such stuff, with all their basting!"

And so he took the well-greased lead
And rubbed it o'er a box of earth
That stood on deck,—a parsnip bed,—
And then he sought the skipper's berth.

"Where are we now, sir? Please to taste."
The skipper yawned, put out his tongue,
Then oped his eyes in wondrous haste,
And then upon the floor he sprung!

The skipper stormed, and tore his hair,
Thrust on his boots, and roared to Marden,
"*Nantucket's sunk, and here we are
Right over old Marm Hacket's garden!*"

James T. Fields.

The

The Description of Castara.

LIKE the violet which alone
    Prospers in some happy shade;
    My *Castara* lives unknown,
To no looser eye betray'd.
      For she's to herself untrue
      Who delights i' th' public view.

Such is her beauty, as no arts
Have enriched with borrowed grace.
Her high birth no pride imparts,
For she blushes in her place.
      Folly boasts a glorious blood,
      She is noblest being good.

Cautious she knew never yet
What a wanton courtship meant:
Nor speaks loud to boast her wit,
In her silence eloquent.
      Of her self survey she takes,
      But 'tween men no difference makes.

She

She obeys with speedy will
Her grave parents' wise commands.
And so innocent, that ill
She nor acts, nor understands.
    Women's feet run still astray
    If once to ill they know the way.

She sails by that rock, the Court,
Where oft honor splits her mast:
And retiredness, thinks the port,
Where her fame may anchor cast.
    Virtue safely cannot sit,
    Where Vice is enthroned for wit.

She holds that day's pleasure best,
Where sin waits not on delight.
Without mask, or ball, or feast,
Sweetly spends a winter's night.
    O'er that darkness whence is thrust
    Prayer and sleep, oft governs lust.

She her throne makes reason climb,
While wild passions captive lie.
And each article of time,
Her pure thoughts to heaven fly.
    All her vows religious be,
    And her love she vows to me.

William Habington, 1605—1654.

A

❧ *A Christmas Carol.*

SO now is come our joyful'st feast;
   Let every man be jolly,
      Each room with ivy leaves is drest,
   And every post with holly.
Though some churls at our mirth repine,
Round your foreheads garlands twine,
Drown sorrow in a cup of wine,
   And let us all be merry.

Now, all our neighbours' chimneys smoke,
   And Christmas blocks are burning;
Their ovens they with baked meats choke, .
   And all their spits are turning.
      Without the door let sorrow lie;
      And if for cold it hap to die,
      We'll bury 't in a Christmas pie,
   And evermore be merry.

Now every lad is wondrous trim,
   And no man minds his labour,
Our lasses have provided them
   A bag-pipe and a tabor;

Young

Young men and maids, and girls and boys,
Give life to one another's joys;
And you anon shall by their noise
Perceive that they are merry.

The client now his suit forbears,
The prisoner's heart is eased;
The debtor drinks away his cares,
And for the time is pleased.
Though other purses be more fat,
Why should we pine or grieve at that?
Hang sorrow! care will kill a cat,
And therefore let's be merry.

The wenches with their wassail bowls,
About the streets are singing;
The boys are come to catch the owls,[1]
The wild mare in is bringing.[2]
Our kitchen-boy hath broke his box,[3]
And to the dealing of the ox
Our honest neighbours come by flocks,
And here they will be merry.

Then wherefore in these merry days
Should we, I pray, be duller?

[1] There was a rural custom in olden time, among the youths, of *hunting owls and squirrels* on Christmas day.

[2] No information can be gained of the nature of this sport.

[3] The old Christmas money-box was made of earthenware, and required to be broken in order to get at the money it contained.

No,

No, let us sing some roundelays,
  To make our mirth the fuller.
    And whilst thus inspir'd we sing,
    Let all the streets with echoes ring,
    Woods and hills and everything
  Bear witness we are merry.

Old Carol, by George Wither, 1622.

MY Lilla gave me yestermorn
    A rose, methinks in Eden born,
    And as she gave it, little elf!
She blush'd like any rose herself.
Then said I, full of tenderness,
    "Since this sweet rose I owe to you,
Dear girl, why may I not possess
    The lovelier Rose that gave it too?"

Unknown.

Nocturne.

❧ *Nocturne.*

BELLAGGIO.

UP to her chamber window
　A slight wire trellis goes,
　　And up this Romeo's ladder
Clambers a bold white rose.

I lounge in the ilex shadows,
I see the lady lean,
Unclasping her silken girdle,
The curtain's folds between.

She smiles on her white-rose lover,
She reaches out her hand
And helps him in at the window—
I see it where I stand !

To her scarlet lips she holds him,
And kisses him many a time—
Ah, me! it was he that won her
Because he dared to climb !

Thomas Bailey Aldrich.

Spectator

¶ *Spectator Ab Extra.*

AS I sat at the café, I said to myself,
    They may talk as they please about what they
    call pelf,
They may sneer as they like about eating and drink-
    ing,
But help it, I cannot, I cannot help thinking
    How pleasant it is to have money, heigh-ho!
    How pleasant it is to have money.

I sit at my table *en grand seigneur*,
And when I have done, throw a crust to the poor;
Not only the pleasure itself of good living,
But also the pleasure of now and then giving:
    So pleasant it is to have money, heigh-ho!
    So pleasant it is to have money.

They may talk as they please about what they call
    pelf,
And how one ought never to think of one's self,

How pleasures of thought surpass eating and drinking,
My pleasure of thought is the pleasure of thinking
>How pleasant it is to have money, heigh-ho!
>How pleasant it is to have money.

LE DINER.

Come along, 'tis the time, ten or more minutes past,
And he who came first had to wait for the last;
The oysters ere this had been in and been out;
While I have been sitting and thinking about
>How pleasant it is to have money, heigh-ho!
>How pleasant it is to have money.

A clear soup with eggs: *voila tout;* of the fish
The *filets de sole* are a moderate dish
À la Orly, but you're for red mullet, you say:
By the gods of good fare, who can question to-day
>How pleasant it is to have money, heigh-ho!
>How pleasant it is to have money.

After oysters, sauterne; then sherry; champagne,
Ere one bottle goes, comes another again;
Fly up, thou bold cork, to the ceiling above,
And tell to our ears in the sound that we love
>How pleasant it is to have money, heigh-ho!
>How pleasant it is to have money.

I've the simplest of palates; absurd it may be,
But I almost could dine on a *poulet-au-riz,*
Fish and soup and omelette and that, — but the
>deuce —

>>>There

There were to be woodcocks, and not *Charlotte Russe!*
    So pleasant it is to have money, heigh-ho!
    So pleasant it is to have money.

Your Chablis is acid, away with the hock,
Give me the pure juice of the purple Médoc;
St. Peray is exquisite; but if you please,
Some Burgundy just before tasting the cheese.
    So pleasant it is to have money, heigh-ho!
    So pleasant it is to have money.

As for that, pass the bottle, and hang the expense —
I've seen it observed by a writer of sense,
That the labouring classes could scarce live a day,
If people like us didn't eat, drink, and pay.
    So useful it is to have money, heigh-ho!
    So useful it is to have money.

One ought to be grateful, I quite apprehend,
Having dinner and supper and plenty to spend,
And so suppose now, while the things go away,
By way of a grace we all stand up and say
    How pleasant it is to have money, heigh-ho!
    How pleasant it is to have money.

PARVENANT.

I cannot but ask, in the park and the streets,
When I look at the number of persons one meets,
Whate'er in the world the poor devils can do
Whose fathers and mothers can't give them a *sous.*
    So needful it is to have money, heigh-ho!
    So needful it is to have money.

I

I ride, and I drive, and I care not a d——n,
The people look up, and they ask who I am;
And if I should chance to run over a cad,
I can pay for the damage, if ever so bad.
    So useful it is to have money, heigh-ho!
    So useful it is to have money.

It was but this winter I came up to town,
And already I'm gaining a sort of renown;
Find my way to good houses without much ado,
Am beginning to see the nobility too.
    So useful it is to have money, heigh-ho!
    So useful it is to have money.

O dear, what a pity they ever should lose it,
Since they are the people who know how to use it;
So easy, so stately, such manners, such dinners;
And yet, after all, it is we are the winners.
    So needful it is to have money, heigh-ho!
    So needful it is to have money.

It's all very well to be handsome and tall,
Which certainly makes you look well at a ball,
It's all very well to be clever and witty,
But if you are poor, why it's only a pity.
    So needful it is to have money, heigh-ho!
    So needful it is to have money.

There's something, undoubtedly, in a fine air,
To know how to smile and be able to stare,
High breeding is something, but well-bred or not,
                            In

In the end the one question is, what have you got?
  So needful it is to have money, heigh-ho!
  So needful it is to have money.

And the angels in pink, and the angels in blue,
In muslins and moirés so lovely and new,
What is it they want, and so wish you to guess?
But if you have money, the answer is yes.
  So needful, they tell you, is money, heigh-ho!
  So needful it is to have money.

Arthur H. Clough.

❧ Stanzas on Woman.

WHEN lovely Woman stoops to folly,
  And finds too late that men betray,
    What charm can soothe her melancholy,
  What art can wash her guilt away?

The only art her guilt to cover,
  To hide her shame from every eye,
To give repentance to her lover,
  And wring his bosom —— is, to die.

From " The Vicar of Wakefield."

To

To Lucasta, on Going to the Wars.

TELL me not, (sweet,) I am unkind,
That from the nunnery
Of thy chaste breast and quiet mind
To war and arms I fly.

True : a new mistress now I chase,
The first foe in the field;
And with a stronger faith embrace
A sword, a horse, a shield.

Yet this inconstancy is such,
As you too shall adore;
I could not love thee, dear, so much,
Lov'd I not Honour more.

From "Lucasta," 1649, by Richard Lovelace.

The

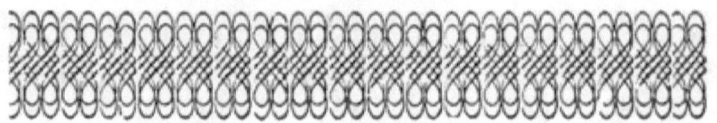

¶ *The Miller of Dee.*

THERE was a jolly miller once
   Lived on the river Dee;
   He worked and sang from morn till
      night,
No lark more blithe than he.
And this the burden of his song
   For ever used to be—
I care for nobody, no, not I,
   If nobody cares for me.

The reason why he was so blithe,
   He once did thus unfold—
The bread I eat my hands have earn'd;
   I covet no man's gold;
I do not fear next quarter-day;
   In debt to none I be,
I care for nobody, no, not I,
   If nobody cares for me.

A coin or two I've in my purse,
   To help a needy friend;
A little I can give the poor,
   And still have some to spend.

Though

Though I may fail, yet I rejoice
　　Another's good hap to see,
I care for nobody, no, not I,
　　If nobody cares for me.

So let us his example take,
　　And be from malice free ;
Let every one his neighbour serve,
　　As served he'd like to be.
And merrily push the can about,
　　And drink and sing with glee ;
If nobody cares a doit for us,
　　Why not a doit care we.

　　　　　　　　　　　　　　Unknown.

🐦 *On His Mistress.*

SHALL I tell you how the rose at first grew red,
　　And whence the lily whiteness borrowèd ?
　　You blush'd, and straight the rose with red was
　　　　dight,
The lily kiss'd your hand, and so was white.
Before such time, each rose had but a stain,
And lilies nought but paleness did contain :
You have the native colour, these the dye,
And only flourish in your livery.

　　　　　　From "Wit's Recreations," 1640.

　　　　　　　　　　　　　　　　An

¶ *An Epitaph upon Husband and*
Wife, who died and were buried together.

TO these whom death again did wed,
   This grave 's the second marriage bed.
   For though the hand of Fate could force
'Twixt soul and body a divorce,
It could not sever man and wife,
Because they both lived but one life.
Peace, good reader, do not weep;
Peace, the lovers are asleep.
They, sweet turtles, folded lie
In the last knot that love could tie.
Let them sleep, let them sleep on,
Till the stormy night be gone,
And the eternal morrow dawn;
Then the curtains will be drawn,
And they wake into a light
Whose day shall never die in night.

               Richard Crashaw, 1616 — 1650.

                      Siren

❧ Siren Pleasant! Foe to Reason.

AN ODE.

NOW I find thy looks were feignèd,
　Quickly lost and quickly gainèd!
　Soft thy skin, like wool of wethers,
Heart unstable, light as feathers;
Tongue untrusty, subtle sighted,
Wanton will, with change delighted:
　　Siren pleasant! foe to reason,
　　Cupid plague thee for this treason!

Of thine eyes I made my mirror,
From thy beauty came mine error,
All thy words I counted witty,
All thy smiles I deemèd pity.
Thy false tears that me aggrievèd
First of all my trust deceivèd:
　　Siren pleasant! foe to reason,
　　Cupid plague thee for this treason!

Feigned acceptance when I askèd,
Lovely words with cunning maskèd.
Holy vows, but heart unholy;
Wretched man! my trust was folly.

　　　　　　　　　Lily

Lily white and pretty winking,
Solemn vows, but sorry thinking:
     Siren pleasant! foe to reason,
     Cupid plague thee for this treason !

Now I see, O, seemly cruel !
Others warm them at my fuel.
Wit shall guide me in this durance,
Since in love is no assurance.
Change thy pasture ! take thy pleasure !
Beauty is a fading treasure :
     Siren pleasant! foe to reason,
     Cupid plague thee for this treason !

Prime youth lusts not age's still follow,
And make white these tresses yellow ;
Wrinkled face for looks delightful,
Shall acquaint the Dame despiteful :
And when Time shall eat thy glory ;
Then, too late, thou wilt be sorry.
     Siren pleasant ! foe to reason,
     Cupid plague thee for thy treason !

          Thomas Lodge, 1556 — 1625.

On

On the Death of a Favourite
Cat, Drowned in a Tub of Gold-Fishes.

'TWAS on a lofty vase's side,
　　Where China's gayest art had dyed
　　　The azure flowers that blow;
Demurest of the tabby kind,
The pensive Selima reclined,
　　　Gazed on the lake below.

Her conscious tail her joy declared:
The fair round face, the snowy beard,
　　　The velvet of her paws,
Her coat that with the tortoise vies,
Her ears of jet, and emerald eyes—
　　　She saw, and purr'd applause.

Still had she gazed; but midst the tide
Two angel forms were seen to glide,
　　　The genii of the stream:
Their scaly armor's Tyrian hue
Through richest purple to the view
　　　Betray'd a golden gleam.

The

The hapless nymph with wonder saw:
A whisker first, and then a claw,
    With many an ardent wish,
She stretched, in vain, to reach the prize,
What female heart can gold despise?
    What cat's averse to fish?

Presumptuous maid! with looks intent
Again she stretch'd, again she bent,
    Nor knew the gulf between.
(Malignant Fate sat by and smiled.)
The slippery verge her feet beguiled,
    She tumbled headlong in.

Eight times emerging from the flood
She mew'd to every watery god,
    Some speedy aid to send.
No Dolphin came, no Nereid stirr'd:
Nor cruel Tom, nor Susan heard —
    A favourite has no friend!

From hence ye beauties undeceived,
Know, one false step is ne'er retrieved,
    And be with caution bold:
Not all that tempts your wandering eyes
And heedless hearts is lawful prize,
    Nor, all that glisters, gold.

            Thomas Gray, 1716—1771.

A

¶ *A Wilful Wife.*

A BALLET.

THE man is blest, that lives in rest
   And so can keep him still.
  And he's accurst that was the first
That gave his wife her will.

What pain and grief, without relief,
  Shall we poor men sustain;
If every Gill shall have her will,
  And over us shall reign.

Then all our wives, during their lives,
  Will look to do the same:
And bear in hand, it is as land
  That goeth not from the name.

There is no man whose wisdom can
  Reform a wilful wife:
But only God, who made the rod
  For our unthrifty life.

Let

Let us, therefore, cry out and roar:
  And make to God request;
That He redress this wilfulness
  And set our hearths at rest.

Wherefore, good wives! amend your lives
  And we will do the same;
And keep not still that naughty will
  That hath so evil a name.

        Old Ballad, from the Cottonian MS.

⤷ *Names.*

I ASKED my fair, one happy day,
  What I should call her in my lay;
    By what sweet name from Rome or Greece;
Lalage, Neæra, Chloris,
Sappho, Lesbia, or Doris,
    Arethusa or Lucrece.

"Ah!" replied my gentle fair,
"Beloved, what are names but air?
    Choose thou whatever suits the line;
Call me Sappho, call me Chloris,
Call me Lalage or Doris,
    Only, only call me thine."

        Samuel T. Coleridge, 1772—1834.

A

ᘒ *A Wish.*

MINE be a cot beside the hill;
   A bee-hive's hum shall soothe my ear;
   A willowy brook, that turns a mill,
With many a fall shall linger near.

The swallow oft beneath my thatch,
   Shall twitter from her clay-built nest;
Oft shall the pilgrim lift the latch,
   And share my meal, a welcome guest.

Around my ivied porch shall spring
   Each fragrant flower that drinks the dew;
And Lucy, at her wheel shall sing
   In russet gown and apron blue.

The village church, among the trees,
   Where first our marriage-vows were given,
With merry peals shall swell the breeze,
   And point with taper spire to heaven.

              Samuel Rogers, 1762—1855.

                              Black-Eyed

¶ *Black-Eyed Susan.*

ALL in the Downs the fleet was moored,
    The streamers waving in the wind,
        When black-eyed Susan came on board:
"O, where shall I my true love find?
Tell me, ye jovial sailors, tell me true,
If my sweet William sails among the crew."

William, who high upon the yard
    Rocked with the billow to and fro,
Soon as her well known voice he heard,
    He sighed and cast his eyes below:
The cord slides swiftly through his glowing hands,
And, quick as lightning, on the deck he stands.

So the sweet lark, high poised in air,
    Shuts close his pinions to his breast
If chance his mate's shrill call he hear,
    And drops at once into her nest:
The noblest captain in the British fleet
Might envy William's lip those kisses sweet.

" O, Susan, Susan, lovely dear,
 My vows shall ever true remain;
Let me kiss off that falling tear;
 We only part to meet again.
Change as ye list, ye winds, my heart shall be
The faithful compass that still points to thee.

"Believe not what the landsmen say,
 Who tempt with doubts thy constant mind:
They'll tell thee sailors, when away,
 In every port a mistress find:
Yes, yes, believe them, when they tell thee so,
For thou art present wheresoe'er I go.

" If to fair India's coast we sail,
 Thy eyes are seen in diamonds bright,
Thy breath is Afric's spicy gale,
 Thy skin is ivory so white.
Thus every beauteous object that I view,
Wakes in my soul some charm of lovely Sue.

" Though battle call me from thy arms,
 Let not my pretty Susan mourn;
Though cannons roar, yet safe from harms
 William shall to his dear return.
Love turns aside the balls that round me fly,
Lest precious tears should drop from Susan's eyes."

The boatswain gave the dreadful word,
 The sails their swelling bosom spread;

No

No longer must she stay aboard;
  They kissed, she sighed, he hung his head.
Her lessening boat unwilling rows to land;
"Adieu!" she cries, and waves her lily hand.

John Gay, 1688—1732.

MYRTILLA, early on the lawn,
    Steals roses from the blushing dawn;
    But when Myrtilla sleeps till ten,
Aurora steals them back again.

Unknown.

AS lamps burn silent with unconscious light,
  So modest ease in beauty shines most bright;
  Unaiming charms with edge resistless fall,
And she who means no mischief does it all.

Aaron Hill, 1685—1750.

IF all be true that I do think,
  There are five reasons we should drink;
  Good wine—a friend—or being dry—
  Or lest we should be by and by—
  Or any other reason why.

Dr. Henry Aldrich, 1647 — 1710.

King

¶ *King Oberon's Apparel.*

WHEN the monthly hornèd queen
  Grew jealous that the stars had seen
  Her rising from *Endymion's* arms;
In rage she threw her misty charms
Into the bosom of the night;
To dim their curious, prying light.
 Then did the dwarfish fairy elves —
Having first attired themselves —
Prepare to dress their *Oberon*, king,
In highest robes, for revelling.
 In cobweb shirt, more thin
Than ever spider since could spin;
Bleached by the whiteness of the snow,
As the stormy winds did blow
It in the vast and freezing air.
No shirt half so fine! so fair!
 A rich waistcoat they did bring,
Made of the trout-fly's gilded wing:
At that, his Elfship 'gan to fret,
Swearing it would make him sweat,

Even

Even with its weight; and needs would wear
His waistcoat wove of downy hair
New shaven from a eunuch's chin.
That pleased him well; 'twas wondrous thin!
    The outside of his doublet was
Made of the four-leaved true-love grass;
On which was set so fine a gloss,
By the oil of crispy moss,
That through a mist, and starry light,
It made a rainbow every night.
On every seam there was a lace,
Drawn by the unctuous snail's slow trace;
To it, the purest silver thread
Compared, did look like dull pale lead.
Each button was a sparkling eye
Ta'en from the speckled adder's fry;
Which in a gloomy night and dark,
Twinkled like a fiery spark.
    And for coolness, next his skin,
'Twas with white poppy lined within.
    His breeches of that fleece were wrought,
Which from Colchus, *Jason* brought;
Spun into so fine a yarn,
That mortals might it not discern;
Woven by *Arachne* in her loom,
Last before she had her doom;
Dyed crimson with a maiden's blush,
And lined with dandely on plush.
    A rich mantle he did wear,
Made of tinsel gossamer;

Bestarred

Bestarred over with a few
Diamond drops of morning dew.
　His cap was all of "lady's love"
So passing light, that it did move
If any humming gnat or fly
But buzzed the air, in passing by.
　About it was a wreath of pearl
Dropped from the eyes of some poor girl;
Pinched, because she had forgot
To leave fair water in the pot.
　And for feather he did wear,
Old *Nisus'* fatal purple hair.
　The sword they girded on his thigh,
Was smallest blade of finest rye.
　A pair of buskins they did bring
Of the "cow lady's" coral wing;
Powdered o'er with spots of jet,
And lined with purple violet.
　His belt was made of myrtle leaves
Plaited in small curious threaves;
Beset with amber cowslip studs,
And fringed about with daisy buds.
In which his bugle horn was hung
Made of the babbling *Echo's* tongue;
Which set unto his moon-burned lip,
He winds; and then his fairies skip.
　At that, the lazy dawn 'gan sound,
And each did trip a fairy round.

From " Musarum Deliciæ," 1656.

The

¶ *The Doorstep.*

THE conference-meeting through at last,
   We boys around the vestry waited
   To see the girls come tripping past,
Like snowbirds, willing to be mated.

Not braver he that leaps the wall
   By level musket-flashes litten,
Than I, who stepped before them all,
   Who longed to see me get the mitten.

But no; she blushed and took my arm!
   We let the old folks have the highway,
And started toward the Maple Farm
   Along a kind of lover's by-way.

I can't remember what we said,
   'Twas nothing worth a song or story,
Yet that rude path by which we sped
   Seemed all transformed, and in a glory.

The snow was crisp beneath our feet,
   The moon was full, the fields were gleaming;

                                        By

By hood and tippet sheltered sweet,
  Her face with youth and health was beaming.

The little hand outside her muff —
  O sculptor, if you could but mould it ! —
So lightly touched my jacket-cuff,
  To keep it warm I had to hold it.

To have her with me there alone,—
  'Twas love and fear and triumph blended.
At last we reached the foot-worn stone
  Where that delicious journey ended.

The old folks, too, were almost home ;
  Her dimpled hand the latches fingered,
We heard the voices nearer come,
  Yet on the doorstep still we lingered.

She shook her ringlets from her hood,
  And with a " Thank you, Ned," dissembled ;
But yet I knew she understood
  With what a daring wish I trembled.

A cloud passed kindly overhead,
  The moon was slyly peeping through it,
Yet hid its face, as if it said,
  " Come, now or never ! do it ! *do it !* "

My lips till then had only known
  The kiss of mother and of sister,
But somehow, full upon her own
  Sweet, rosy, darling mouth,— I kissed her !
                                    Perhaps

Perhaps 'twas boyish love, yet still,
    O, listless woman, weary lover!
To feel once more that fresh wild thrill
    I 'd give—but who can live youth over?

                    Edmund Clarence Stedman.

 *Song.*

WITH an honest old friend and a merry old song,
    And a flask of ¦old¦ port, let me sit the night
        long,
And laugh at the malice of those who repine
That they must drink porter, whilst I can drink wine.

I envy no mortal tho' ever so great,
Nor scorn I a wretch for his lowly estate;
But what I abhor and esteem as a curse,
Is poorness of spirit, not poorness of purse.

Then dare to be generous, dauntless and gay,
Let us merrily pass life's remainder away;
Upheld by our friends, we our foes may despise,
For the more we are envied, the higher we rise.

                    Henry Carey, 16—— 1743.

                                    Pratt's

Pratt's Astral Oil

IS THE BEST ILLUMINATING OIL FOR FAMILY USE

THAT is manufactured from Petroleum. It is perfectly safe, and may be burned in the ordinary Kerosene Lamp, or in the more elaborate and costly Student and Drawing-Room Lamps. During the many years that we have been manufacturing it, not an accident is known to have resulted from its use. Considering that the sales of ASTRAL OIL amount to many millions of gallons annually, it will be evident how superior is its quality, and how great the care observed in its distillation. In many households here and in foreign countries, the ASTRAL OIL is used with confidence and enjoyment where any other oil would not be tolerated. For the convenience and protection of the consumer, we pack the ASTRAL OIL in tin cans of one, two and five gallons capacity, these in turn being boxed for shipping. Each can has our seal over the opening, that the buyer may be guaranteed against adulteration.

We invite correspondence, and shall be pleased to give further information as to prices and terms upon application.

Pratt's

Pratt's Patent Prepared Gasolene

IS a *strictly pure and uniform* article which we have been manufacturing largely for many years, and which may be relied on to be the best ever offered for making gas. The fact that we are supplying fully four-fifths of the entire quantity consumed in this market and abroad is proof of the truth of this assertion and of the great excellence of these goods. Manufactured with the utmost care, and after the most approved processes, we confidently recommend it to all those who make use of gas-machines and wish the best article of GASOLENE.

Owners of mills and factories, proprietors of hotels, etc., lighting their premises by this method, as well as families having country residences, will find it to their advantage to use this GASOLENE, and thus save themselves the expense and inconvenience likely to result from the use of a poor or uncertain quality of gasolene.

We fully understand the requirements of customers, and guarantee entire satisfaction.

Orders for the PATENT PREPARED GASOLENE may be sent direct to us, or it may be obtained from our authorized agents at various points.

Double-Deodorized

Double-Deodorized Benzine and Naphtha.

WE wish to call particular attention to our make of the above products, of all gravities from 62° to 76°, all of which are twice distilled and extra deodorized, making them absolutely pure and sweet, and especially suited for the manufacturing of Rubber Goods, Varnishes and Japans, Dryers, Ready-mixed Paints, Floor Oil-Cloths, Window Shades, Enameled Cloths; as well as for Dyers, Furniture, Carpet, Clothing, or Glove Cleaners, and for all who use Benzine and Naphtha for any purpose whatever, and desire a really superior article. We are prepared to furnish these goods in any quantity from one barrel upward, and are confident that all who are critical as to quality will be pleased with them.

BOULEVARD GAS FLUID.—We make a special grade of Naphtha (under this name) for use in what are known as Naphtha or Vapor Burners for Street lamps—a large number of which are now used in lighting the Streets of many cities and towns, here and abroad.

Pratt's

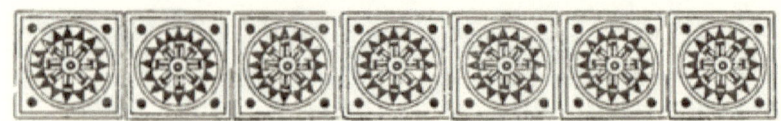

Pratt's Astral Oil

HAS been in general use for over thirteen years, and to a larger extent than all similar grades of Oil combined.

Its reputation is world-wide, and it will not be questioned that for family use it is the *safest* Oil, as well as being in all other respects superior to any product of petroleum ever made for illuminating purposes. The only obstacle heretofore to its universal use — its slightly higher price as compared with that of ordinary burning Oil — is now to a great extent removed, as the lower price of the crude material, together with our improved processes of manufacture, enables us to sell it at less than half the price at which it was originally put on the market. The essential features of the ASTRAL — which have made its reputation — *absolute safety*, *perfect burning qualities*, and *freedom from disagreeable odor*, will be fully maintained in the future as in the past.

The ASTRAL OIL may be obtained from almost any dealer in the United States, and from our authorized agents in Canada and Europe.

Gentle

GENTLE READER: Here we must take our leave of thee—but before saying Adieu, allow us to express the hope that our labour has afforded thee some little pleasure; and, if this be so, that we and our agents shall receive in return thy patronage and good wishes.

We desire, also, to acknowledge our obligations to the well known publishing house of Houghton, Mifflin & Co. for having most generously permitted us to print herein several poems by American authors, the copyrights of which they own.

Farewell! and Merrie Christmas!